BEAR GOES TO TOWN

Anthony Browne

DOUBLEDAY

NEW YORK   LONDON   TORONTO   SYDNEY   AUCKLAND

Also by Anthony Browne
THE LITTLE BEAR BOOK

Published by Doubleday, a division of
Bantam Doubleday Dell Publishing Group, Inc.
666 Fifth Avenue, New York, New York 10103

Doubleday and the portrayal of an anchor with a dolphin
are trademarks of Doubleday, a division of
Bantam Doubleday Dell Publishing Group, Inc.

Library of Congress Cataloging-in-Publication Data
U.S. CIP data applied for

RL: 2.2
ISBN 0-385-26524-7 (Trade)
ISBN 0-385-26525-5 (Library)

One day Bear went to town.

There were a lot of people rushing about. It was
rush hour. Bear was small and people could not
see him. They knocked him down.

Bear saw big yellow eyes looking down at him.

"What is that?" asked Cat, looking at Bear's pencil.

"It's my magic pencil," said Bear.

"Then draw me something to eat," said Cat.

Bear drew lots of different kinds of food.
"Will that do?" Bear asked.
"Yes, thank you," said Cat and gobbled
everything up.
Bear and Cat stood outside a butcher's shop.

Bear did not like the look of the butcher.

Bear and Cat stood outside a bear shop.
"I wonder if people eat them," thought Bear.
Look out, Cat!

HELP . . . !

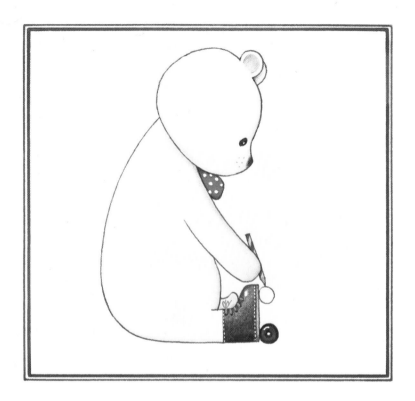

Cat was thrown into a van. Bear drew himself a pair of roller skates and hurried after him.

The van turned into a gateway and stopped in a yard.

The driver locked Cat in a shed.
"Mmmm. Most odd," muttered Bear. As the
guard's back was turned, Bear went round to the
side of the building and drew himself a ladder.

Bear got to work with his pencil again and sawed through the bars on the shed window.

He climbed in.

"You took your time," Cat said.

"What is this place?" Bear asked.
"We don't know," said Cow, "but can you get us out?"

Bear used his pencil. "Follow me," he said.

Sheep refused to leave.

STOP!!!

Guards chased the animals across the yard.

"Banana skins, I think," said Bear and began to draw.

Whoooooooops.

Look out behind you, Bear!

"Tacks, I think," said Bear and drew some.

Psssssssss.

The animals got away.

"Where are we?" asked Rooster.

"In the middle of nowhere," Bear replied.

"I like it here," said Pig.

"We don't want to be eaten . . ."

". . . or beaten," added Dog.

"Yes, it's a dog's life," sighed Cat.

"Easy," said Bear and began to draw.

"Thank you, Bear."

And Bear walked on.